S0-CNG-549

Topic: Interpersonal Skills **Subtopic:** Empathy

Notes to Parents and Teachers:

As a child becomes more familiar reading books, it is important for them to rely on and use reading strategies more independently to help figure out words they do not know.

REMEMBER: PRAISE IS A GREAT MOTIVATOR!

Here are some praise points for beginning readers:

- I saw you get your mouth ready to say the first letter of that word.
- I like the way you used the picture to help you figure out that word.
- I noticed that you saw some sight words you knew how to read!

Book Ends for the Reader!

Here are some reminders before reading the text:

- Point to each word you read to make it match what you say.
- Use the picture for help.
- Look at and say the first letter sound of the word.
- Look for sight words that you know how to read in the story.
- Think about the story to see what word might make sense.

Words to Know Before You Read

adventure

explore

forest

friends

laugh

shadows

walk

werewolf

How to Be Friends with This Werewolf

By Erin Savory
Illustrated by Ana Zurita

Rourke Educational Media
A Division of Carson Dellosa Education

I met Walda in the forest.

Walda is a werewolf.

She loves to explore.

She loves the moon.
It makes her feel safe.

Sometimes she gets scared.

How can I be friends with this werewolf?

We explore together.
We use our maps.

There is adventure ahead!

We find a cave.

It is dark.
Walda cannot see the moon.

This is scary!

I sing silly songs to make her laugh and make funny shadows with my hands.

She is not scared anymore.

We walk to a river.
I'm afraid of water.

Walda helps me.
I am not afraid anymore.

Want to be friends with this werewolf?

Come to the forest.

Walda is ready for adventure!

Book Ends for the Reader

"I know..."

What does Walda like to do?

"I think..."

How does Walda help when her friend is scared?

What happened in this book?

Look at each picture and talk about what happened in the story.

About the Author

Erin Savory is a writer who lives in Florida. She loves to paint with her two-year-old son. She loves spending time in nature. Reading is her favorite activity.

About the Illustrator

Ana Zurita was born by the sea in Valencia, Spain, where she completed her studies in Fine Arts and currently lives with her wonderful family. She is a big fan of the beach in winter, the color yellow, the smell of old books, and heavy blankets. But what has made her the happiest from a very early age is drawing. That's why her greatest dream is to make others happy with her illustrations.

Library of Congress PCN Data

How to Be Friends with This Werewolf / Erin Savory
(How to Be Friends)
ISBN 978-1-73164-347-6 (hard cover)(alk. paper)
ISBN 978-1-73164-311-7 (soft cover)
ISBN 978-1-73164-379-7 (e-Book)
ISBN 978-1-73164-411-4 (ePub)
Library of Congress Control Number: 2020945146

Rourke Educational Media
Printed in the USA
01-0592313123

© 2021 Rourke Educational Media

All rights reserved. No part of this book may be reproduced or utilized in any form or by any means, electronic or mechanical including photocopying, recording, or by any information storage and retrieval system without permission in writing from the publisher.

www.rourkeeducationalmedia.com

Edited by: Tracie Santos
Layout by: Morgan Burnside
Cover and interior illustrations by: Ana Zurita